Harry
the Highlander

This book belongs to

....

To my youngest son Nathan, who, from a very young age, has shown great interest in my work and who has inspired me to write this story.

Designed by County Studio International Ltd

Printed in China

Published by

GW Publishing
An Imprint of Lomond Books Ltd.
13-14 Freskyn Place
East Mains Industrial Estate
Broxburn
EH52 5NF

www.gwpublishing.com
www.lomondbooks.com

ISBN 978-0-9570844-7-6

Harry
the Highlander

Up the Glen

Written by Cameron Scott Illustrated by Cee Biscoe

Harry was sad to see his mum leave for the Highland Show.

He was missing her already, even though she had not quite left yet.

She was taking part in a **BIG** competition for the best-looking cow, and Harry was sure she would win the **top prize** with her beautiful coat.

He was a very brave little calf and had told his mum that he would be okay. He would just play with the other young cows in the field.

However, Harry was a **Highland cow** with a very shaggy coat and looked different from all the other cows.

And , just because he looked different, they would not play with him, so Harry wandered off to a far corner of the field to be by himself.

No one else visited this corner of the field, so no one had noticed the broken-down wall.

Harry decided this was his chance to get away from the unfriendly cows and maybe even find some friendly ones... some that were more like him.

He **climbed** through the gap in the wall and set off up the glen.

It wasn't long before he came across a tiny brown mouse that looked rather sad.

"Hello," said Harry. "Why are you so glum?"

The little mouse told him that his whiskers were too **spikey** and *tickled* the other mice while they tried to sleep.

They wouldn't let him sleep with them anymore, so the tiny brown mouse had decided to look for some friends that didn't mind his long whiskers.

"Well," said Harry, "you can come with me if you want."

"My coat is so **thick** that your whiskers won't **tickle** me."
The mouse scampered up onto Harry's back
and the two young animals
headed up the glen.

As they were resting by a riverbank they heard a strange **SKWaK-SKWaKiNg** sound. An adorable little duckling was swimming up the river, all by herself.

"Hello," said Harry.
"Where are you going?"

The duckling told them that the other ducks wouldn't let her sing because she couldn't quack properly. She had waddled off to sing by herself. "Well," said Harry, "you can come with us if you want. We would love to hear you."

The three new friends continued together up the glen, singing and SKWaKiNg along the way.

Harry had been telling his new friends how unkind the other cows had been to him when they came across a shy young fox cub sitting by an old tree.

"Hello," said Harry. "Why are you here all alone?"

The little fox
said the other
foxes would not let
him eat with them because his **long** nose
kept getting in the way. He had
decided he would try and find some friends
that didn't mind how **long** his nose was.
"Well," said Harry, "we don't mind at all."
And the four unlikely friends wandered on even
further up the glen.

The higher they went, the colder it became and everyone huddled closer to Harry. Suddenly, as they made their way around some big boulders,

skwak

they bumped into a rather odd looking creature.

"I'm sorry," said the bumbling little goat. "I'm always **BUMPING** into things."

"That's okay," replied Harry. "What are you doing all the way up here?"

"The other goats say I'm too clumsy, and told me to keep out of their way."

Harry said, "You can come along with us if you like. We won't mind if you **BUMP** into us."

The five unusual friends stuck even closer together as the wind blew harder, but still they pushed on, right to the top of the glen.

By the time they got to the top it was **VERY COLD**. It was also getting dark and the friends were now very tired.

"It's too late to go back down now," said Harry. "We'd better find somewhere safe and warm for the night."

They soon found a small cave just big enough to squeeze inside, and they **huddled** together out of the cold.

Harry told them how happy he was to have found so many new friends.
"I suppose we are all a bit different," he said, "but that doesn't matter."

Before long, they were fast asleep, cuddled up beside Harry.

keeping warm with the help of his **thick shaggy** coat.

While they were fast asleep, it snowed... and it snowed... and it snowed. Snuggled up close to Harry inside the cave, the animals were safe and warm, but...

...when they woke up the next morning it was white everywhere... everywhere except inside the cave, which was still dark.

The snow had piled up at the entrance, and had trapped them all inside.

The shy young fox cub sat up.

He sniffed and he sniffed again, trying to find the entrance to the cave.

Then he poked & poked with his **long** nose, until he made a small hole to the outside.
  "Well done" said Harry. "You're a really **wise fox**."

Outside, everywhere was covered in snow.

Even though it was *magical* and they all wanted to play for a while, the five friends agreed they had better head back to the farm.

As they made their way back
down the glen, they came to a very wide river.
"Look, the bridge is **broken**," said the tiny
mouse. "I can't swim across there."

"Neither can I," said the wise young fox. "We'll be washed away." But the bumbling little goat had an idea!

She **chewed** and **chewed** and **chewed** her way right through the rope from the old bridge.

"What a **clever goat**," said Harry. "But how will that help us to cross to the other side?" he asked.

"I've got an idea!" said the little duckling. She grabbed the rope and jumped into the water.

She **splashed** and she **spluttered**, she **splattered** and she **struggled**, and eventually she made it across to the other side.

"You are a plucky **little duck!**" shouted Harry, as she wrapped the rope around a big rock as tight as she could.

Then, the tiny brown mouse scampered along the rope.

After that,
Harry held on
to the rope and the clever goat and
the not-so-shy fox held on to each other
as they made their way carefully across.

They all gave their coats a good shake. Harry
gave his **shaggy** coat an extra shake because it
was so **thick** and **heavy** with water.
"Which way now?" he asked, as they looked
at the wall of trees.

Suddenly, the tiny brown mouse scampered up
to the top of the tallest tree.

"I can see a farm,"
he shouted.
"I can show you the way."

Then, the **daring mouse** climbed up on Harry's back, and led them through the woods and down the glen.

Harry's mum was waiting, and very pleased to see him with all his new friends.

"We are all a bit different, but that's what makes us special," she explained. "If you're friendly, you will always make new friends."

And with that, the farmer agreed they could all stay with Harry on the farm.